Dear Parent:

Congratulations! Your child is taking the first steps on an exciting journey. The destination? Independent reading!

STEP INTO READING® will help your child get there. The program offers books at five levels that accompany children from their first attempts at reading to reading success. Each step includes fun stories, fiction and nonfiction, and colorful art. There are also Step into Reading Sticker Books, Step into Reading Math Readers, and Step into Reading Phonics Readers— a complete literacy program with something to interest every child.

Learning to Read, Step by Step!

Ready to Read Preschool–Kindergarten
• big type and easy words • rhyme and rhythm • picture clues
For children who know the alphabet and are eager to begin reading.

Reading with Help Preschool–Grade 1
• basic vocabulary • short sentences • simple stories
For children who recognize familiar words and sound out new words with help.

Reading on Your Own Grades 1–3
• engaging characters • easy-to-follow plots • popular topics
For children who are ready to read on their own.

Reading Paragraphs Grades 2–3
• challenging vocabulary • short paragraphs • exciting stories
For newly independent readers who read simple sentences with confidence.

Ready for Chapters Grades 2–4
• chapters • longer paragraphs • full-color art
For children who want to take the plunge into chapter books but still like colorful pictures.

STEP INTO READING® is designed to give every child a successful reading experience. The grade levels are only guides. Children can progress through the steps at their own speed, developing confidence in their reading, no matter what their grade.

Remember, a lifetime love of reading starts with a single step!

www.stepintoreading.com

Educators and librarians, for a variety of teaching tools, visit us at
www.randomhouse.com/teachers

Library of Congress Cataloging-in-Publication Data
Kulling, Monica.
Go, Stitch, go! / by Monica Kulling ; illustrated by Denise Shimabukuro and the Disney storybook artists.
    p.   cm. — (Step into reading. A step 2 book)   summary: A Hawaiian girl's new dog is actually an alien, and two strange creatures have come to earth to catch him and take him to jail.
ISBN 0-7364-1350-2 (trade) — ISBN 0-7364-8010-2 (lib. bdg.)
[1. Extraterrestrial beings—Fiction.   2. Pets—Fiction.   3. Fugitives from justice—Fiction.
4. Hawaii—Fiction.]
I. Shimabukuro, Denise, ill.   II. Title.   III. Series: Step into reading. Step 2 book.
PZ7.K9490155   Go   2003   [E]—dc21   2002014520

Printed in the United States of America   14 13 12 11 10 9 8 7 6 5

DISNEY'S
Lilo & Stitch

Go, Stitch, Go!

By Monica Kulling

Illustrated by Denise Shimabukuro and
the Disney Storybook Artists

Designed by Disney's Global Design Group

Random House 🏠 New York

Lilo waved to Myrtle.

She wanted to be

Myrtle's friend.

"I got a new dog!"

Lilo yelled.

"His name is Stitch."

Myrtle rode up
on her new trike.
"Wow!" said Myrtle.
"That dog is ugly."
Stitch made a face.

Stitch was <u>not</u> a dog.

He was blue and furry.

He had big ears.

And he had sharp teeth.

Stitch was really
an alien!

Pleakley and Jumba
were aliens, too.

They had come to Earth
to catch Stitch.
Pleakley tripped over
Jumba's foot.
"Whoa!" said Pleakley.

Stitch saw Pleakley.

Then he saw Jumba.

He had to get away!

Stitch had an idea.

He grabbed
Myrtle's trike.

He grabbed Lilo's hand.

They took off!

Stitch rode fast!

"Hey!" yelled Myrtle.

"Oh, no!" said Pleakley.
"Stitch is getting away!"

"Grab that scooter!"

said Jumba.

"We will catch him!"

Lilo and Stitch rode
under a waterfall.
Splash!

They got all wet.

But Lilo did not care.

"Cool!" she cried.

Jumba and Pleakley
rode under
the waterfall.
They got soaked.

They did not like it
one bit!

Stitch came to a cliff.
There was nowhere to go.
Just lots and lots
of water.

Stitch turned right.

Lilo hung on tight.

Jumba and Pleakley
zoomed right into
the water!
Lucky for them,
someone was surfing!

Lilo and Stitch
zoomed right
through a market!
"Yum!" said Lilo.

"Ooof!" said Pleakley.
Jumba drove into
a bunch of bananas!

Stitch rode past
a volcano.

It began to rumble.

Smoke and

lava came out.

"Uh-oh!" said Lilo.

"Go, Stitch, go!"

Stitch rode faster.

"We have him now,"
said Jumba.
The aliens
were getting closer.

But so was
the lava!

Jumba and Pleakley
jumped off the scooter.
They climbed a tree.

And Lilo and Stitch
got away!

"That sure was fun!"
said Lilo.
"Let's do it again!"